John A. Symonds

Waste

a lecture delivered at the Bristol institution for the advancement of

science, literature, and the arts, on Tuesday, February the 10th, 1863

John A. Symonds

Waste
a lecture delivered at the Bristol institution for the advancement of science,
literature, and the arts, on Tuesday, February the 10th, 1863

ISBN/EAN: 9783337406479

Printed in Europe, USA, Canada, Australia, Japan

Cover: Foto ©Andreas Hilbeck / pixelio.de

More available books at **www.hansebooks.com**

WASTE:

A

LECTURE

DELIVERED AT THE

BRISTOL INSTITUTION

FOR

THE ADVANCEMENT OF SCIENCE, LITERATURE AND THE ARTS,

ON

TUESDAY, FEBRUARY THE 10TH, 1863,

BY

JOHN ADDINGTON SYMONDS, M.D., F.R.S.,ED.,

FELLOW OF THE ROYAL COLLEGE OF PHYSICIANS,
CONSULTING PHYSICIAN TO THE BRISTOL GENERAL HOSPITAL, ETC., ETC.

LONDON:

BELL AND DALDY, 186, FLEET STREET.

1863.

SYLLABUS.

Waste of solid substance of the Earth—surface of mountains—coasts—rocks,—from sea-waves—rainfalls, &c.—pp. 1—10.

Waste of Vegetable Life—struggle for existence—depredations of animals—accidents.—pp. 10—12.

Waste of Animal Life—by human agency—waste in geologic periods.—pp. 12—15.

Waste of Human Life —by natural agents — pestilence and war—destruction of aboriginal races—waste of human capabilities.—pp. 15—22.

Waste of the Works of Man — cities — libraries — literature. —pp. 22—28.

Questions and Reflections. —pp. 29—36.

Compensations.—pp. 36—48.

Waste viewed as transmutation.—pp. 48—51.

LECTURE ON WASTE.

———— - ————

IT WOULD not be in accordance with your feelings or my own, were I to commence the business of this evening without making reference to the great loss which this Institution has so recently sustained in the death of our venerated President, the MARQUIS OF LANSDOWNE. That event has cast a shade over far wider spheres than this. The gloom has been felt in the Senate, and in her Majesty's Council, and it has spread over the whole nation; but it is not wonderful that the loss should be specially felt in an Institution which has for so many years derived honour and encouragement from the prestige of that illustrious name. I am not so presumptuous as to think of attempting to pronounce LORD LANSDOWNE'S eulogy, though I might be prompted to say something from the fact that I had the privilege of enjoying his Lordship's acquaintance; for with that largeness of heart, which was one of his prominent characteristics, he extended his friendship from the very highest in the land to the most humble. Many worthy tributes have been already offered to his memory, and there are more to come. Many eloquent voices, many brilliant pens will be ready to set forth and record what HENRY, MARQUIS OF LANSDOWNE was as a public man, as one of the leaders of a great political party, as a Senator, a Councillor, a Minister of State;—but it is not fitting that in an Institution devoted to science, literature, and art, silence should be altogether kept, when science, literature, and art have lost one of their most enlightened cultivators, one of their most munificent patrons, one of their most ardent friends. We in this Institution, in particular, must lament his death, but we must also feel thankful that he was so long spared to us. LORD LANSDOWNE was elected President in the year 1836, so that our Institution had the benefit of his protection and patronage for nearly thirty years.

I need not say more—to say more would be ill-timed and impertinent—but I could not well say less; and I proceed, therefore, to the Lecture, the subject of which, and I trust the tone of it also, will not be altogether out of harmony with the thoughts and feelings which must arise in our minds, when we consider how much of highest talent and culture, how much experienced statesmanship, how much knowledge and wisdom, how much taste and refinement, how much worth, nobleness, and goodness, have been lost to the world—how much happiness and enjoyment to a vast circle of admiring and loving friends—how much honour and countenance to ourselves—by that event to which I have thus made so slight and inadequate an allusion.

To THE student of Final Causes there are no facts in nature that on a first view present more difficulties than those which belong to decay and destruction. Fertile lands in a very few hours overspread by a desolating inroad of the sea, on the retreat of which, if ever it does withdraw, there is left for a time a sandy, stony desert ;

plants of exquisite organisation springing above the soil and dying undeveloped; forests and prairies consumed by fire; myriads of animals, multitudes of human beings perishing in full life and strength: these and many like facts are at first sight startling. The mighty, ever-teeming mother Earth—is she thwarted by some malignant power in her schemes of beneficence? or, by some blind law of productiveness, does she go on for ever throwing off her wonderful progeny, careless, when they have left her bosom, whether they live or die, or what ultimate destiny awaits them?

But we will not now ask questions. Let us survey in detail a few of the phenomena of waste, and either when they are under our eyes, or when we are recalling them, some obvious enquiries will suggest themselves.

Among the fragile forms of the animated world around us, one is so used to the sight of destruction, that the questions alluded to are almost less likely to arise than when, by some accidental circumstance, we become aware of decay among objects which had seemed to be fixed and enduring. I shall not easily forget the impression made upon me one day, when I stood for the first time in a

scene of savage grandeur, which is, I dare say, well
known to many of this audience—the upper region of the Mer de Glace. It was the early morn-
ing ; some golden light had just begun to shoot
into the deep indigo of the sky above the mountains in the east; and while I was endeavouring
to grasp the more salient points of that wonderful scene, fearing lest some essential element of
its sublimity might be overlooked, my attention was caught by sounds of crashing, unlike
the solemn peals with which distant avalanches
announce their descent, and I asked the guide
what was the cause of those sounds. He told
me, with the indifference of a person to whom
that which I enquired about was a matter of daily
routine, that it was only the breaking and falling down of masses of rock in the mountains.
And there, assuredly, as I looked up towards the
rugged peak of the Charmoz, and observed atten-
tively the different slopes, I could see masses of
stone continually tumbling down;—small enough
in the distance, but quite discernible;—and every
few seconds or so, the sound was repeated. Now
the obvious thought that arose was, — if those
sounds, or, rather, the causes of them, were always

going on, was not that mountain falling away piecemeal, and destined to leave its giant limbs in the valleys, which would, in time, be no longer valleys, but plains? The peaks and the ridges looked so broken and jagged and splintery against the sky, that, with that sound constantly in one's ears, it was difficult to avoid expecting that they might snap off before our eyes;—forgetful for a moment of the vast dimensions of what looked like needles and sword-blades. I know not whether those peaks and ridges have really had any of their lines and angles altered since they were first accurately observed; but we may be certain that, whether their chief features have changed or not within the records of human generations, those everlasting hills are everlasting only to the bodily eye of man, that cannot see changes on so large a scale, and that they are surely wasting and crumbling to decay.

But any one who has observed the *moraine* of a glacier might interpose,—Surely it is not necessary to strain the eyes to the mountains themselves, when, immediately at their feet, proofs of destruction or disintegration are visible in blocks of granite, some of immense size, either still resting on the ice, or left on the sides of the ice-river along which the glacier once descended, but from which it has of late years withdrawn,—leaving, however, these proofs of its gigantic powers both of support and of conveyance.

Striking as is this work of demolition in stupendous masses of the earth's substance, there is not less sure a work of destruction effected, though in a somewhat less imposing way, by rivers that are perpetually wearing down the surfaces which they traverse, and carrying the results of their attrition to the plains below. Rain-falls even have their effects, and sometimes on a large scale, as when by sudden condensation of great masses of vapour the mountain torrents are enormously swollen. Such rocks as the stratified horizontal sandstone may in this manner be reduced to sand and gravel by the flooded streams. Sir. C. LYELL, describing the action of such rain-falls on the south face of the Khasia, or Garrow Mountains in Eastern Bengal, says "so great is the superficial waste or denudation, that what would otherwise be a rich and luxuriantly wooded region is converted into a wild and barren moorland."

Mr. JUKES, in an opening address before the Geological Section of the British Association at Cambridge (1862), when speaking of the wearing down force exerted by rains, gave as an instance the loss of altitude sustained by the great limestone range of the south of Ireland, a loss computed to be as much as from 300 to 400 feet.

The waste of land in landslips is too well known for us to dwell upon it, as well as the corroding effect of the sea on shores. In certain situations on the eastern and southern coasts of our own island, the signs of such destruction are but too obvious. When the shores consist of brittle, crumbling substances, as in the tertiary strata, such effects do not surprise one. But the harder and more resistent rocks are not safe from the devastations of the ocean. On the northern coasts of Great Britain may be seen some very striking remains of rocks that would *a priori* have seemed invulnerable. Granite, gneiss, mica-slate, serpentine. greenstone, porphyry, stand in broken masses, with rent and angular forms, that attest in a wild picturesque manner the terrible battering to which they have been subjected by the violence of the Atlantic waves urged on by westerly gales.

In some parts the inroads of the sea are made comparatively easy by the decomposition of soft granite. When the waves have once had access by such means, they are not slow to improve their opportunity, and they widen the breach by rude mechanical force. But even without this preliminary sapping, the sea will battle against a rampart of porphyry, "with all the force of great artillery," says Dr. HIBBERT, till it has forced an entrance.*

The wasting power of water is exhibited in one part of Europe in forms most strange and fantastic. In Saxon Switzerland, as it is called, or rather miscalled, you look down from a wooded height into a valley filled with rocks, which, to the dullest imagination, call up the images of castles, pillars, obelisks, broken colonnades, rude sculptured tombs, and every species of ruin or rough-hewn work in stone that the eye may have ever seen. These singular forms are the remnants of basaltic rocks, which have in geologic periods been rudely dealt with by waters, eaten into, worn down, battered and broken.

* See LYELL's "Elements of Geology," p. 300.

The desolations from igneous forces, whether let loose on the surface of the earth from the fiery mouths of volcanoes, or pent up in the interior, and made manifest in earthquakes, belong to the veriest commonplace of devastation, and need only this passing allusion.

The waste of organic forms and of their life is exemplified in that group of phenomena, which Mr. DARWIN has so well described as resulting from the struggle for existence. "We behold the face of nature," he says, "bright with gladness, and we often see superabundance of food; we do not see, or we forget, that the birds which are idly singing round us mostly live on insects or seeds, and are thus constantly destroying life; or we forget how largely these songsters, or their eggs, or their nestlings, are destroyed by birds and beasts of prey." He tells us how seedlings are destroyed in vast numbers by various enemies; for once on a small piece of ground he found that out of 357 seedlings no less than 295 were destroyed. The more vigorous plants destroy the weaker ones, even when fully grown; "thus out of twenty species growing on a little plot of turf (three feet by four), nine perished from the other species being allowed to grow up freely."

Destruction on a large scale is effected by predatory animals. It has been calculated that were sportsmen to remain idle for a season there would be no increase of game, unless the gamekeepers were constantly on the watch to destroy vermin. Inclemencies of season work great havoc; sometimes directly, by cutting off a supply of food, but still more so indirectly, by increasing the competition with other species. How vegetable growths may be kept down and seem to disappear under the destruction of animals, is strikingly shown by the effects of enclosure. I remember noticing many years ago in the Highlands of Scotland, at Pitlochry, near the pass of Killicrankie, that though the profusion of birch trees in some situations indicated that they were indigenous, yet the partiality of their distribution seemed opposed to the idea, for they were wanting on large tracts that appeared to present the same soil, the same substrata, and the same qualities of atmosphere. It was explained to me by my friend Professor FORBES that the differences depended on enclosure, and that it would be only necessary to fence in a piece of ground so as to prevent the access of cattle, and birches would shew themselves in abundance. When Mr. DARWIN's book came into my hands, I was interested in finding that this naturalist had made a like observation as to fir trees.*

Very extensive destruction is sometimes brought on the vegetable world by accidents, or by the carelessness of man. Thus, one has read of grass-land on fire over miles of plain, and of vast forests laid waste in the same manner; the combustion having arisen from neglect in extinguishing a fire that had been used by some wandering tribe or party of travellers.

Animals are extinguished on a large scale by human agency. "That the extinction of many of the existing races of animals must soon take place," says Dr. MANTELL, "from the immense destruction occasioned by man, cannot admit of doubt. In those which supply fur, a remarkable proof of this inference is cited in a late number of 'The American Journal of Science.' Immediately after South Georgia was explored by Captain Cook, in 1771, the Americans commenced

* "Origin of Species," p. 71.

carrying seal skins from thence to China, where they obtained most exorbitant prices. *One million two hundred thousand skins* have been taken from that island alone since that period; and nearly an equal number from the Island of Desolation! The number of the fur seals killed in the South Shetland Isles (s. lat. 63°,) in 1821 and 1822, amounted to three hundred and twenty thousand. This valuable animal is now almost extinct in all these islands. From the most authentic statements it appears certain that the fur trade must henceforward decline, since the advanced state of Geographical Science shows that no new countries remain to be explored. In North America the animals are slowly decreasing, from the persevering efforts and the indiscriminate slaughter practised by the hunters, and by the appropriation to the use of man of those forests and rivers which have once afforded them food and protection."[*]

But all instances of destruction of vegetable and animal life on the present surface of the earth are as nothing, compared with the evidences presented in older strata. It would be incredi-

[*] Dr. MANTELL's "Wonders of Geology," vol. i., p. 101.

ble, had we not unequivocal proof given to the senses, that there had been such extensive destruction of vegetable forms as the coal measures reveal : the coal itself being, as you know, the product of the decomposition of coniferous plants. As to animal life, it is enough to think of the extensive coral reefs and islands built up by animals; and of mountains nearly composed of the debris of animals, as in the oolite which runs through a great part of Europe, and of the enormous collection of encrinitic remains in the mountain-limestone.

And almost everywhere we find the debris of living forms scattered, or densely packed in their stony beds, to a degree that makes the earth seem a great collection of catacombs — a vast necropolis. It is by a strong effort of the imagination that we conceive those strata to have been once scenes of beauty and verdure and luxuriance, shadowed by stately palms, and populous with animal tribes ; and it is rather a painful effort to reflect on the ruin and desolation and destruction that overtook creatures into which God had breathed the breath of life, however little else there may have been in these beings to excite our sympathy. In our own experience we see only the destruction of individuals, however numerous, the species still remaining ; but the palæontologist discovers that in the worlds under his survey Nature was scarcely more conservative of species than of individuals.

> So careful of the type! but no,
>> From scarped cliff and quarried stone
>> She cries—" A thousand types are gone !
> I care for nothing; all shall go."

And how has man been wasted! I will not here say how he has been wasted by himself,— by his own folly and wickedness ; nor how he has been wasted by his fellow-man,—by greed and recklessness and oppression and cruelty. But he has seemed to be wasted by the elements,— by agencies over which human will and human thought could have no control : starved by the failure of crops, poisoned in marshes and jungles, swept away by floods, swallowed up by earthquakes, consumed by the lava, or choked and buried in the ashes of volcanoes, drowned in angry or perfidious seas, and, above all, smitten by those unseen angels of death whose wings are spread on mysterious pestilences.

As to the scale on which human beings have perished from the last-named cause, we may instance the devastation of the Black Plague, in the fourteenth century. Here are one or two items taken from HECKER's "Epidemics of the Middle Ages," p. 23:—

In Florence died of the Black Plague	...	60,000
" Venice	...	100,000
" Marseilles, in one month	... ...	16,000
" Sienna	...	70,000
" Paris	...	50,000
" St. Denys		14,000
" Avignon	...	60,000
" Strasburg		16,000
" Lübeck	...	9,000
" Basle	...	14,000
" Erfurt, at least...	...	16,000
" Weimar	..	5,000
" Limburg		2,500
" London, at least ...	...	100,000
" Norwich	...	51,100
To which may be added —		
Franciscan Friars in Germany ..	...	124,434
Minorites in Italy	...	30,000

In many places in France not more than two out of twenty of the inhabitants were left alive, and the capital felt the fury of the plague alike in the palace and the cot.

* * * * * * * * * * * *

The churchyards were soon unable to contain the dead, and many houses left without inhabitants fell to ruins. In Avignon, the Pope found it necessary to consecrate the Rhone, that bodies might be thrown into the river without delay, as the churchyards would no longer hold them ; so, likewise, in all populous cities, extraordinary measures were adopted, in order speedily to dispose of the dead. In Vienna, where for some time 1200 inhabitants died daily, the interment of corpses in the churchyards and within the churches, was forthwith prohibited, and the dead were then arranged in layers, by thousands, in six large pits outside the city, as had already been done in Cairo and Paris.—*Ibid.*, p. 25.

I have said that I would not speak of that destruction of man which has come from the will of man ;—else what waste might appear before us in the carnage of battles, the slaughter of storm and sack, wholesale murders by wicked kings, wholesale butcheries by savage mobs, and the torturing deaths instigated by fanatical and malignant priests. But one cannot wholly exclude wars from the category of those desolations which fall upon man against his will, when one thinks by how few minds and hands some of the most devastating wars have been directed.

When 60,000 soldiers lay stretched on the frozen plain of Eylau, and nearly a like number under a scorching sun on the field of Wagram, it cannot be said that, though struck down in war, they were the victims of their own violent passions.

C

They lay there stiff in death, or writhing in anguish, because the ambition of one man willed it;—the heart of one man was reckless of the amount of suffering and misery and death, at which he purchased his ends, provided only he did attain them. Had a plague swept over the Palatinate, the people could not have been less the authors of their own calamities than they were, when the savage soldiers of DURAS obeyed the orders issued from the *salons* of Versailles, with the consent of that bigoted voluptuary who boasted of his descent from ST. LOUIS. And, indeed, in almost all wars but those of a purely defensive kind (and this exception applies to one side only) we must put the destruction of human life under the head of Waste; and I know not what other term will do so well for the heaps of skeletons which in our own time have encumbered the Khyber Pass, or which are strewn round the walls of Sebastopol, and still more for the corpses now rotting on the plains of Virginia.

Let us think, too, of the disappearance of whole races of mankind; and what havoc must have been made by the inroads of stronger races trampling down the weak,—driving them from their hunting fields, planting them out from their pastures, exterminating them by the cruelties, the diseases, the vices of civilised nations : — worse still, some of these civilised nations (for example, the Spaniards in America,) smiting them down with the cross, in practical blasphemy of that symbol of love and pity. Even in our own milder times, there has been enough of extermination to make philanthropists set on foot a society, for the protection of aboriginal races.

These are some instances of one kind of waste of human life : but there is another view which indicates enormous waste, simply in the undeveloped potentiality of man. If we look over the map of the world, and consider how long it has been peopled, and how richly, and then consider what man now is, and how little he has attained to, comparatively, can we avoid thinking of waste ? History tells us what myriads lie buried in the old Greek and Roman lands, and in all our modern Europe. Something, too, we know of the human relics that are blown about in the desert dust of Egypt and Palestine. Asia, mother of the nations, bewilders

the imagination that tries to call up the series
of races that, according to the most limited
chronology, have hung on her mighty breast.
Whoever has dared to push towards the pesti-
lential interior of that quarter of the world, the
fringe only of which, till in these latter days,
travellers have been contented to touch, has
found human life ever teeming, ever exhaust-
less: while, in what we call the New World,
cities actually overgrown by ancient forests, and
remains of old polities long worn out, and traces
of a civilization which it must have taken ages
to accomplish, and which it has taken ages to
efface, tell how man there, too, has abounded.
I say nothing of the tribes now dimly looming
through the mists which have enveloped the
primeval anthropology of the earth, but which
have had some light thrown upon them by the
combined researches of the antiquarians and
naturalists of these latter days. Every part of
the survey increases our awe, and brings back
on us a humiliating feeling of ignorance, far
surpassing that which ensues on the contemplation of fossil infusoria and fossil saurians.
We are sure, from various evidences, that it

must have been all for ultimate good: how, we know not. Allow that the intellectual, and moral, and religious development of one race, is no measure for that of another, and that the capacities and susceptibilities in these respects are not equal nor alike; still in the lowest types of man there are germs of powers, possibilities of being, enough to make the inevitable question start to the mind,—what have all these men and women done since they breathed the breath of life? These countless tribes, with their quick senses, their nimble apprehensions, their marvellous hands, their erect stature, their "large discourse of reason," and their shaping fancies; what have they done in proportion to their numbers? Alas! the "vanity of vanities," which the preacher so mournfully ejaculated nigh three thousand years ago, was but another formula for what we are trying to discourse of under the category of Waste.

And yet something has been done; one race has given monuments to all succeeding ages of the height to which philosophy, and poetry, and art can rise: another of the power which men may attain by force of law and patriotism, and political organization; another of the gifts of God in the endowment and development of religious sense and religious knowledge; and the men of the present time have learned wonderful mechanical arts, and the virtues of social love and social compassion.

Yes, something has been done in some parts of the world. But, alas! of that which has been done how much has perished! Cities innumerable have been absolutely swept away, and of the greatest the remains are meagre;—Babylon and Nineveh marked only by mounds, till the genius and industry of this age disinterred some wonderful relics; Thebes, with comparatively few fragments of temples, and obelisks, and sphinxes, and gigantic statues, yet unburied by the sand; Athens, not even the skeleton of its former strength and beauty, but with only a mutilated member here and there; and Rome, standing on the ruins of at least three predecessors; more, perhaps, lying buried beneath than has since stood above, even when that, of which so little is left, was unimpaired. To these the least instructed in history will be able to add a long catalogue of other cities, of which a few present picturesque

remains like Baalbec and Palmyra, others that
survive only in their names, others with so little
remaining except their names, that, like the
Ephesus of Mr. FALKENER, it is only to be re-
constructed by means of the utmost ingenuity,
fortified by all the resources of archæological
knowledge, and artistic skill, and classical
scholarship. But long lists of names of cities
might be culled from ancient authors which
are literally dead names, not having one single
association in our minds, at least in ordinary
minds. And, again, figures might be brought
forward recounting the numbers of cities, the
names of which have vanished even from the
countries where they stood. It is an old lament,
the lament over perished cities. Listen, for one
moment, to this from the preface to Burton's
" Anatomy of Melancholy ":—

Tell me, politicians, why is the fruitful Palestina, noble Greece,
Egypt, Asia Minor, so much decayed, and (mere carcases now)
faln from what they were ?   The ground is the same ;—but
the government is altered ; the people are grown slothful, idle ;
their good husbandry, policy and industry is decayed.   *Non
fatigata aut effeta humus* (as COLUMELLA well informs SYLVINUS)
sed nostrâ fit inertiâ, &c. May a man believe that which ARIS-
TOTLE, in his Politicks, PAUSANIAS, STEPHANUS, SOPHIANUS, GER-
BELIUS, relate of Old Greece ?   I finde heretofore 70 cities in

Epirus (overthrown by PAULUS ÆMILIUS), a goodly province in times past, now left desolate of good towns, and almost inhabitants ;—62 cities in Macedonia, in STRABO's time. I find 30 in Laconia, but now scarce so many villages, saith GERBELIUS. If any man, from Mount Täygetus, should view the countrey round about, and see *tot delicias, tot urbes per Peloponnesum dispersas*, so many delicate and brave built cities, with such cost and exquisite cunning, so neatly set out in Pelepounesus, he should perceive them now ruinous and overthrown, burnt, waste, desolate, and laid level with the ground. *Incredibile dictu*, &c. And as he laments, *Quis talia fando, Temperet a lachrymis? Quis tam durus aut ferreus* (so he prosecutes it), who is he that can sufficiently condole and commiscrate these ruins? Where are those 4000 cities of Egypt ; those hundred cities in Crete? Are they now come to two? What saith PLINY and ÆLIAN of Old Italy? There were, in former ages, 1166 cities : BLONDUS and MACHIAVEL both grant them now nothing near so populous and full of good towns as in the time of AUGUSTUS (for now LEANDER ABERTUS can find but 300 at most), and, if we may give credit to LIVY, not then so strong and puissant as of old : *" They mustered 70 legions in former times, which now the known world will scarce yield.* ALEXANDER built 70 cities in a short space for his part : our Sultans and Turkes demolish twice as many, and leave all desolate. Many will not believe but that our island of Great Britain is now more populous than ever it was ; yet let them read BEDE, LELAND, and others ; they shall finde it most flourished in the Saxon Heptarchy, and in the Conquerours time was far better inhabited, than at this present. See that *Doomsday Book;* and shew me those thousands of parishes, which are now decayed, cities ruined, villages depopulated, &c.

But all such destruction points mainly to the waste of the larger works of man's hands, though there was indeed much of other waste, — much waste of the arts and the products of the arts that made life happy and enjoyable, and that elevated and embellished it—(as for instance what sculptures demolished, what frescoes effaced!)—and the loss of the genius and knowledge and skill which planned those cities, with all their towers and domes and temples, their theatres and palaces. But there has been still greater waste of thought in the lost literature of the world,—partly because the characters cannot be read, still more because the records are gone,—the books have perished. And it is a melancholy reflection that vast stores of knowledge so painfully hived up, that finest gems of thought so carefully polished, so carefully set, should have been not merely lost by the accidents of time, but should have also been recklessly and blindly destroyed by the animosity of hostile nations and hostile creeds.

"The literary treasures of antiquity," says Mr. D'ISRAELI, " have suffered from the malice of men, as well as that of time. It is remarkable that conquerors, in the moments of victory, or in the unsparing devastation of their rage, have not been satisfied with destroying *men*, but have even carried their vengeance to *books*. The Romans burnt the books of the Jews, of the Christians, and the Philosophers; the Jews burnt the books of the Christians and the Pagans; and the Christians burnt the books of the Pagans and the Jews. The greater part of the books of ORIGEN and other heretics were continually burnt by the orthodox party." GIBBON pathetically describes the empty library of Alexandria, after the Christians had destroyed it. "The valuable library of Alexandria was pillaged or destroyed; and near twenty years afterwards the appearance of the empty shelves excited the regret and indignation of every spectator, whose mind was not totally darkened by religious prejudice. The compositions of ancient genius, so many of which have irretrievably perished, might surely have been excepted from the wreck of idolatry, for the amusement and instruction of succeeding ages; and either the zeal or avarice of the Archbishop might have been satiated with the rich spoils which were the reward of his victory."

But the waste of disuse suggests reflections scarcely less mournful. Have you not felt when pacing along the galleries of great libraries, glancing from side to side at the labels and names on those piled up treasures, with their blazonry as faded and pale as the escutcheons in the adjoining churches,—have you not felt that those titles to immortality (for such the poor departed authors in the pride of their hearts conceived them to be), were, after all, the most impressive lessons that could be taught of the transitoriness of human glory, of the vanity of human expectations? It is sad to walk in a churchyard over the graves of nameless dead,—it is sadder to walk through cloisters of venerable colleges and cathedrals, and to see on the foot-worn pavement, and on the walls laden with pompous monuments, the names of men who, for all that we or thousands like us know about them, might just as well have been nameless. In vain does the poor weak voice cry out from the tomb, *siste viator!* We do not stop, for why should we? the tenant's name is nothing to us. We linger only a moment to admire the turn of phrase in the panegyric, or even, alas! only to smile at its quaint conceits; and if a serious thought comes over us it is not for those unknown dead, but for the sadness of the common doom that involves the hopes and joys and labours of all our race,—*quam vanæ sint spes quam fluxa sint hominum gaudia,*—"how vain the hopes of men, how fleeting are their joys." And so, I say, it is very mournful to glance at those unknown names and titles in our great libraries, which, indeed, are great cemeteries; and there lie the authors with all their glorious thoughts, their fine moralizings, their convincing arguments and eloquent admonitions, all coffined in the very volumes that were to keep them ever living; and the titles on the labels are little better than epitaphs, and for all that they bring to our minds. there might as well have been only a simple "*Hic jacet.*"

Such thoughts as these give us hints of the waste of oblivion. We just descry the objects before they are finally drawn behind the impenetrable curtain. But who shall conjecture what great, and heroic, and beneficent beings, what glorious and beautiful works, have been gathered into the eternal darkness, leaving not one wreck or token to tell the after ages how woeful has been their loss?

Under the term Waste, I have included the premature decay, or the destruction of that which has seemed to have a definite work to fulfil, or a definite place in the order and constitution of the universe. Instances have arisen before our minds in the perishing of organic forms before they have matured, in human beings cut off in their prime, in the destruction of human works, in the breaking up of parts of the material fabric of the world. We have seen enough to prove that such phenomena, anomalous as they at first sight appear, are too numerous to be regarded as exceptional. Such seeming chaos must somehow belong to the universal kosmos, for there is a continuity in the disruptions, a constancy in the changes, a sort of rhythm in the discords. Change is the soul of the world; all things are in flux, and there is nothing stationary but in the thought of man. He sees the seed sprout, and the stem spring up, and the flower blossom, and the seed form and fall, and he thinks that this is to happen over and over again in the same order. If in reality he saw the same things and the same forces at work, he would assuredly see the same results. for no one will dispute that the same antecedents will beget the same consequents. But he is in reality looking at different things, which only seem to be the same.

The faith in nature, and in her constancy and perfection, according to man's notion of constancy and perfection, leads to many errors of inference. The prevalence of definite forms in organic life has much to do with the idea in question. Yet how often is this same work of nature incomplete. You can scarcely find a plant with every leaf or petal perfect, — scarcely an animal in which there is not some defect, however trifling. The soil and the atmosphere, to which the seed and the animal are indigenous, are a part of nature, as well as the organic beings in question ; but the one often does not bear, and the other is cut off immature. Such facts belong as much to the system of nature, as the perfect organisms growing and flourishing, and they all come under the law of change and transmutation ; and if we could see all, we should perceive that out of the decay and death life was ever springing. Individual leaves, or blossoms, or seeds, or whole plants, may fail ; but look at the ever-returning wealth of foliage, and the never failing flowers, and the teeming produce, and the swarming flocks and herds! The contingencies of blight and decay and destruction are provided against by a productiveness that will more than compensate for such losses. And those casualties, disturbing and distracting as they seem, would, if traced along their several lines and clusters of causes, be seen to bear the same order and arrangement as the phenomena which we more easily apprehend ; and we should find all subordinated to laws of change, revolution, motion. The member must shrink, or be cast off, for the sake of the individual form ; and the individual form goes for nothing in comparison with the species ; and the species must end, when the time is come for the conditions of its existence to be altered.

Lightning and tempest—volcanoes and earthquakes—fog and frost—drought and deluge—dearth and blight and poison—old age, disease and death,—all belong to the same plan as sunshine, dews, and showers; and verdure, bloom, and vintage ; and youth and health and strength and beauty.

It is the shortness of our time on earth, the

limitation to our own powers of production, that
makes us stand aghast at the contemplation of
what we call waste. We propose to ourselves
definite ends,—and for these we work, and design, and plan, and go through endless perplex-
ities, and encounter endless obstacles; and if all
our deliberations and contrivances and resolves and
exertions fail in their purpose, we feel that our
thought and care and toil have been spent in vain.
And our hearts, as well as our minds and hands,
may be disappointed. Ambition frustrated, hopes
defeated, affections bereaved or blighted,—these,
too, cause man to say,—Why all these throbbings,
and agitations, and dreamings, and yearnings, if
they were to come to nothing? Would it not
be better not to feel, than to look back on such
profitless expenditure of feelings—"the weary
chase the wasted hour!" But man sees not as
God sees.

> "The One remains,—the many change and pass,—
> Heaven's light for ever shines, earth's shadows fly;
> Life, like a dome of many colour'd glass,
> Stains the white radiance of eternity."

But the discontent of man comes from his
greatness as well as from his littleness. It is

because he has done so much with so much
strength and skill, that he is vexed that the work
of his hands does not always accomplish his wishes,
or that, when they have been completed, still the
works are not abiding. Lord of Nature and her
finite beings, subjugating the qualities of matter
and the forces of matter to his will and purpose;
creating nothing, but taking command of the
powers of nature and compelling them to work
under new combinations, so as to supply his
wants, and augment his pleasures, and gratify
his pride; and dealing with form and colour and
sound, so that things in the outward world shall
be copies of the ideas in his mind, and present
to other men, and for ages on ages, the same
thoughts and feelings which he was the first to
conceive; he is dissatisfied when, in the courses of
time, and the fatal conjunctures of chance, the
things which he had bound together fall asunder,
and the old undisciplined forces of nature resume
their sway, and the primitive combinations of
elements return to what they were, before he
took possession of them, and set them in new
places, and gave them new work and new
functions; and he is mortified because his webs are

unwoven, and his compositions dissolved, and his forms effaced; and he sighs out his "vanity of vanities," as if he had a right that his works should abide for ever. And from this state of feeling he is apt when looking at the works which are none of his, to transfer his sentiments, or to extend his sympathy to the gods themselves; for he mourns over the waste of the riches, and over the losses and destruction and decay of the works of nature, as if they were his own. But this superfluous lamentation and compassion comes from his shortsightedness.

In the processes of nature we must look beyond the seemingly marked divisions. These are mere resting places for mortal thought. Combinations and compositions are but for a time. The elements, of which they are made, arrange themselves ever anew. The form seems to vanish, but its essence has not melted away; it has become another, it is transformed.

Is it asked, why were not things differently adjusted? Why the struggle for life? Why so precarious a dependence on the elements? Why those fatal competitions and conflicts? Why the ineffectual battle of the weak with the strong? Why should the mights almost always become the rights? Why such profuseness in production, only to provide for the certainty of failure and extinction? Why should humanity have been made so prone to multiplication, that in order to maintain a due proportion to the means of subsistence, there must be reductions by such terrible processes as war, pestilence, and famine? These and a thousand like questions are the absurd and unprofitable speculations of human ignorance.

If, with our limited range of view, standing, as we do, on so very low a terrace for any prospect of the universe,—if even so standing and looking, we can discover a predominance of good over evil, and discern that some of the works of ravage and dissolution lead on to happiness and beauty, we ought to be content and believe that it is so with all. And the more we reflect, the more we shall be convinced that the waste, over which we mourn, is not really waste but transformation, the most striking type of which is seen in the mutual changes of the great forces of nature; heat passing into electricity, this into chemical attraction, and this into mechanical motion, and this again back into heat and light. For these forces are ever vanishing, ever re-appearing, ever destroyed yet ever preserved, going through endless phases of regenesis by virtue of their reciprocal convertibility.

Moreover, if we review, though hastily, the ground which has been traversed, we shall perceive that, in some instances, phenomena, which appeared at first sight very disastrous, are balanced by compensations, or prove to have been of only temporary duration. The fabric of the solid earth may be broken and dissolved in one part, but it is built up and added to in another. The rivers that rush down the mountain, ploughing it or planing it away, are elsewhere "sowing the continents to be." "The mud, sand, and other detritus," says Dr. MANTELL, "thus produced, are reconsolidated by certain chemical changes which are in constant activity, both on the land and in the depths of the ocean, and new rocks are thus in progress of formation." "Elevations and subsidences," says Dr. BUCKLAND, "inclinations and contortions, fractures and dislocations, are phenomena which, although at first sight they present only the appearance of

disorder and confusion, yet, when fully under-
stood, demonstrate the existence of order, method
and design, even in the operations of the most
turbulent among the many mighty physical
forces, which have affected the terraqueous globe."

Again, while the sea makes such encroach-
ments on the land as we noticed in the earlier
part of the lecture, we know, on the other hand,
that it retires from other shores, leaving vast
tracts of fertile land reclaimable by man's industry; and there are names on our maps, which
tell that the towns which bore them were once
sea harbours, though now lying far inland.

The very deaths of plants must give life to
innumerable other forms; and our artificial
systems of fertilization obviously consist in making
use of the remains of organic beings which
have perished. But all examples of such con-
version of loss into gain shrink in extent before
the great carboniferous deposits. Those spoils
of ancient forests were transported to lakes
and estuaries, and there buried, or, we should
rather say, stored up in subterranean treasure-
houses for the future use of man, and then by a
series of volcanic revolutions lifted up to within

his reach. It was not for nothing that the grand and stately forests of palms were sepulchred in the depths of the earth. But for all that enormous destruction, where would have been the blazing hearths of England?—where those wonderful changes, social and national, that are involved in the mechanical applications of steam?

In adducing some striking instances of the devastations of pestilence, we went back to the fourteenth century. There have been many terrible plagues since that Black Plague, and the cholera of our own time is not to be forgotten. But still there has been a notable though a gradual diminution of such visitations. The steady progress of improvement in sanitary knowledge and sanitary practice, at least in Europe, has abated much of the virulence of the diseases that were formerly so destructive. And the great triumphs of JENNER's discovery are never to be kept out of view, though one of the very effects of it has been that of removing from sight the signs of the existence of that evil which his genius and perseverance taught man to avert. Of many diseases the mortality has been greatly reduced by the advance of science; and even as to epidemics, though, when they have come, they have been apt to exact their dues, with a frightful rigour, from those who have fallen within their power; yet there is good reason for believing, that in the progress of social improvements they will find fewer and fewer subjects.

The lost literature of the world, as we glanced at it, seemed a woeful illustration of waste. But as to even this deprivation we can discern some topics of solace and reconcilement. Of what has perished it is probable that a large part was not worth preserving; another part having fulfilled its temporary function has died away; and of another part it may be said, that what was really valuable in it has been insensibly gathered into the collective thought of educated minds. There have been books which were valuable for the knowledge they contained; but their essence has long since been distilled and absorbed into the general knowledge of mankind; and the original sources are objects of curiosity rather than of use. This may be said of nearly all the literature of science. But the case is different in regard to those writings, the excellence of which consists in the beauty of their composition. The loss of these we must regret, like that of fine paintings and sculptures, the form and colour of which are essential to their character. The truths which NEWTON discovered would remain with us, if his "Principia" and other treatises had sunk in that fatal river of Time, which, LORD BACON tells us, drowns what is weighty and precious, and floats down only what is light and worthless. But if the actual Odyssey, and Hamlet, and Paradise Lost, were gone, no one could tell another what they were. The words themselves in their collocation are as essential as the thoughts; the form is no less indispensable than the substance. But such works form but a small proportion of great libraries. And of that small proportion, comparatively little can be enjoyed by even industrious students, distracted as they must be by the ever increasing literature of the times they live in. Nor is it needful to think only of this prolific age, with its journalism ever presenting new and stronger claims on attention. More than two centuries ago literature seemed redundant.

In 1632 (says Mr. MASSON, in his life of MILTON) just as

now, people complained of a plethora of books. "Good God," says WITHER, in his *Scholar's Purgatory*, "how many dung-boats full of fruitless volumes do they yearly foist upon his Majesty's subjects ; how many hundred reams of foolish, profane, and senseless ballads do they quarterly disperse abroad."— (Vol. i. p. 510.)

And Sir THOMAS BROWNE expresses a like feeling :—

I have heard (he says) some with deep sighs lament the lost lines of CICERO ; others with as many groans deplore the combustion of the library of ALEXANDRIA ; for my own part I think there be too many in the world, and could with patience behold the urn and ashes of the Vatican, could I, with a few others, recover the perished leaves of SOLOMON. * * * * 'Tis not a melancholy *utinam* of my own, but the desires of better heads, that there were a general synod ; not to unite the incompatible differences of religion, but for the benefit of learning, to reduce it, as it lay at first, in a few and solid Authors ; and to condemn to the fire those swarms of rhapsodies begotten only to distract and abuse the weaker judgments of scholars, and to maintain the trade and mystery of Typographers.—(Relig. Med. sec. 24.)

It is curious to notice the different aspects under which the waste of literature appears to the same person at different times. I have quoted GIBBON's lamentation over the first destruction of the library of ALEXANDRIA by a Christian Bishop. With his usual partiality he speaks more leniently of the second destruction by the Mahometans :—

I sincerely (he says) regret the more valuable libraries which have been involved in the ruin of the Roman Empire; but when I seriously compute the lapse of ages, the waste of ignorance, and the calamities of war, our treasures rather than our losses are the objects of my surprise. Many curious and interesting facts are buried in oblivion; the three great histories of Rome have been transmitted to our hands in a mutilated state; and we are deprived of many pleasing compositions of the lyric, iambic, and dramatic poetry of the Greeks. Yet we should gratefully remember, that the mischances of time and accident have spared the classic works to which the suffrage of antiquity had adjudged the first place of genius and glory; the teachers of ancient knowledge, who are still extant, had perused and compared the writings of their predecessors; nor can it fairly be presumed that any important truth, any useful discovery in art or nature, has been snatched away from the curiosity of modern ages.

As to the destruction of races of men, it may console us to bear in mind, that if the individual man must not repine at changes which, though they ruin him, add to the happiness of multitudes of his fellowmen, it cannot be our duty to mourn over the disappearance of races, which have been superseded by others, of higher endowments and larger capacities. The modes in which they have perished, or been absorbed, or amalgamated, may have been painful to contemplate; but those dreadful facts belong to the category of questions for which, as we have already hinted, there is at present no solution,—there being no rest for the perplexed, inquiring mind, but in the belief that they belong to the working of a Divine plan of the universe that must end in good, though in an unknown way. And even with our present perceptions, and powers of understanding, if we survey the countries where such changes of inhabitants have taken place, I cannot imagine that anyone would desire that those changes should be reversed. The Mohawk and the Chippewa may be fine figures for the imagination; and stirring tales may be told of their strength of limb, and marvellous quickness of eye and ear, and of their love of justice, and of their possession of some few domestic virtues, and some shadowy notions of religion; but who would wish them to return to their hunting grounds with their painted skins, and their tomahawks and scalping knives, or even with their rude implements of the chase and their primitive wigwams, and to occupy these regions where another race, however intrusive in the first instance, has now spread fields of waving corn, and scattered the land over with smiling homesteads, and built great cities with churches

and colleges and halls of state, and introduced
the ennobling sciences and refining arts of the
highest civilization achieved by man? ·No.
Alas! for the poor Aborigines! Alas! for their
struggle for existence, their pangs, their heart-
breakings, their many miseries! They must go;
"some natural tears we shed, but wipe them
soon." They must fall under the general law.
So vanished the Canaanites before those wondrous
Children who were to be the learners and
teachers of the best and purest religion mankind has known. So vanished the Pelasgians before the Hellenes, who were to be the authors
of the profoundest philosophy, and the creators of
the highest poetry and the finest arts. So
vanished the Etrurians, and Oscans, and Um-
brians, before the race that was to teach
law, and political organization, and scientific
warfare. So vanished the allophyllian races of
our northern Europe, before those branches of
the great Aryan stock, who brought the useful
arts, the mechanical inventions, the comforts
of life, and, in the fulness of time, and under
the inspiration of Christianity, the mitigations
of suffering, the sympathy for the afflicted,

the pity for the poor, and the sorrow for the sinful, embodied in the hospitals and asylums and reformatory institutions of our modern life.

And with such reflections in our minds we cannot mourn over the waste of the old cities. They are gone. Be it so. Would you build up Thebes again? and again see the worship of the cat, and the cow, and the ibis, even allowing that such superstitious practices were symbolical of esoteric doctrines highly abstract and spiritual? Would you raise up ancient Rome, and recall her Romans, with their cruel, pitiless conquests, their insulting triumphs, their butcherly and debasing sports? One would rather have even modern Rome with her spies, and her dungeons; for the misery she inflicts by her bigotry and tyranny, is at least on a smaller scale.

But Athens—could we recover Athens from the wreck, would it not be a temptation to wish the order of changes rolled back to what she was, when Pericles ruled the destinies of grander intellects, finer fancies, more cunning hands, more delicate senses. more eloquent tongues than the world has known before or since.

Had we the architects and sculptors, would we
not rebuild her Parthenon and Erectheum, repair
and set up again her Theseus and Ilissus, and
all "those forms that mock the eternal dead
in marble immortality," and bid her sages once
more "walk the olive grove of Academe," and
recall the silent voices of her orators and poets?
No; it is better as it is. Fancy must not be
allowed to dazzle the eyes of our judgment
with the picture of that city;

> "A city such as vision
> Builds from the purple crags and silver towers
> Of battlemented cloud, as in derision
> Of kingliest masonry."

We must not forget what was wanting to her
citizens, and which we now possess, with our
riper civilization, our advanced sciences, our
mighty arts, our purer morals, our holier
religion. One thought alone is enough to
make us acquiesce even in the ruin of ancient
Athens. While knowledge and wisdom were
embodied in Pallas Athenè, and much that
was charming was represented by Aphroditè,
yet those higher sentiments and associations

which arise in *our* minds with the name of woman, were not in the minds of the Greeks. Centuries upon centuries of confusion, and misery, and darkness, had to pass over "poor humanity's afflicted will," before that beautiful phase of our modern life was evolved, which represents the ideas contained in chivalry, and the acknowledgment by man of that softening, elevating, and refining process, which he owes to the purer soul, and the more loving heart of woman. This the Greeks had not; so let them go, and their peerless city with them.

If we could, we would not have them again; nor can we join with SCHILLER in wishing to revive their beautiful mythology. Rather would we apostrophise their gods in the language of one of our own poets :—

> " Very pale ye seem to rise
> Ghosts of Grecian deities !
>   *   *   *   *   *
> Gods bereaved, gods belated,—
>   With your purples rent asunder !
> Gods discrowned and desecrated,
>   Disinherited of thunder !
>   *   *   *   *   *

> Get to dust, as common mortals,
> By a common doom and track !
> Let no SCHILLER from the portals
> Of that Hades call you back,—
> Or instruct us to weep all
> At your antique funeral.
>
> PAN, PAN is dead ! "

Were it merely to indulge our curiosity, one would like to reanimate the dwellers in such cities as those of old Etruria, about whom we know so little. But they are gone; they have had their day and their place. As to all that is gone from the world, there must have been a reason for its departure as well as for its coming. Death is in the scheme of the universe no less than life. So we must be content to say with solemn reverence,—

> " Let the dead past bury its dead."

Could we from some far-off extra-mundane station look at events which near at hand seem so disastrous,—all the destruction and havoc and desolation in the world,—they would, probably, under so different an angle of vision, assume an entirely different aspect. The whole system of things being one of unceasing change and flux, such terms as death, and waste, and wreck, and ruin, would lose their significance; they would melt into ideas of unfolding, disintegration, repulsion, and separation; links in that great chain which is also made up of works of development, attraction, composition, and formation, which are for ever going on, since motion is the ultimate law of the universe. The mutations in the solid fabric of the earth, whether gradual or abrupt, at which our imagination is so much amazed and almost frightened, would look like undulations, heavings, and subsidences,—dissolving views of a sublime order of changes; the replacement of old cities by new would appear as little more than kaleidoscopic recombinations; and the busy, striving, toiling, battling tribes of men, falling away here and re-appearing there, would harmonize with the varying scenes of the vegetable world,—the uprooting of forests,—the springing of flowers, and herbs, and crops, and plantations, where once were desert plains or monotonous prairies,—and the rising of lovely islands from the bosom of the barren sea.

And all would be seen as order, growth, development, in the midst of disruption, disintegration, and decay. Under our limited powers of observation, the shifting atoms of organic forms are so insensibly replaced by like atoms, in like combinations, that perfect similarity is mistaken for identity. The rosy cheek of youth, and the brilliant eye of beauty, are undergoing perpetual dissolution and recomposition in the midst of their health and loveliness. With vision microscopically sharpened, we should at every moment discern, in the marvellous processes of cellular life, destruction, decay, and separation, alternating with repair, and growth, and re-union. And so the great globe itself, which to our mortal survey seems covered and confused with waste, and wreck, and ravage, may to the mental eye, removed far off by imagination, or by philosophic abstraction, present only the varying phases of renovation and reproduction, which are ever prevailing over inevitable revolutions and destructions.

All the teachings of experience, and all the divinations of analogy, lead us to believe that those chances and changes and metamorphoses

will ever eventuate, sooner or later, in something
better and nobler; and that the new earth and
the new Heavens which the highest and purest
minds have been inspired to look for, and to
prefigure in solemn vision, will infinitely surpass
in beauty and glory all those which have gone
before them.

ARROWSMITH. PRINTER. QUAY STREET, BRISTOL.